The Frog Prince

Story by:
Wilhelm and Jacob Grimm

Adapted by:
Margaret Ann Hughes

Illustrated by:

Russell Hicks	Lorann Downer
Theresa Mazurek	Rivka
Douglas McCarthy	Matthew Bates
Allyn Conley-Gorniak	Fay Whitemountain
Julie Ann Armstrong	

This Book Belongs To:

Use this symbol to match book and cassette.

nce upon a time there lived a king, a queen and a princess named Laura. Now Laura had a round, golden music box that she had played with ever since she was a little girl.

One day, Laura took her music box to the garden and placed it on the edge of a wishing well. She turned the golden key on the music box, and it began to play the most beautiful music!

Laura danced around the well while the music played. But as she twirled around, Laura bumped the music box, and… it fell into the well!

Just then, a small green frog jumped onto the wall of the well. His name was Pembroke.

Oh, the poor princess! She was so upset. Pembroke felt sorry for Laura, and he offered to help her.

In exchange for saving the music box, Pembroke asked that Laura promise to be his friend. She must play with him all day long,

let him eat food from her plate, and then let him
sleep on her soft satin pillow at night.

Laura did not like making a promise she wasn't sure
she could keep…he was a frog after all. But she
didn't want to lose her music box
either, so she agreed.

Pembroke jumped into the icy cold water
in the well and dove toward the reflection of the
music box. He struggled to bring it to the surface.

Laura lowered the water bucket into the well.
And with all his might, Pembroke pushed the music
box into the bucket, and Laura pulled it up out of
the well.

Laura ran to the castle carrying her music box.
She forgot all about Pembroke down in the well
and about the promise she had made.

That evening in the castle, the royal family sat at a very large table, having dinner. The king and queen talked about the day's events, while Laura sat very quietly. The music box sat on the table, safe and dry. Laura had completely forgotten about the frog.

Just then, there came a light tapping on the castle door.

The guard pulled open the door, and in hopped… Pembroke!

The princess was horrified! Surely he hadn't been serious, but there he was…and ready to eat dinner! The frog jumped onto the table and made his polite introductions to the king and the queen. Then Pembroke turned to Laura and again reminded her of the promise.

Pembroke hopped over to Laura's plate and tied a napkin around his neck. Then he smiled... and waited.

Laura told the king and queen about the music box, the well, and the promise.

The king, being a wise man, decided that Laura should learn the importance of making and keeping a promise. He insisted that Laura do all the things the frog requested. So, Pembroke sat next to Laura and ate from her plate. Laura did not feel like finishing her dinner, and it wasn't long before she decided it was time to go to bed.

The princess kissed her father and mother goodnight and quietly tiptoed away. Pembroke quickly hopped after the princess.

Laura turned around and saw the frog.

She made a most unpleasant face, picked Pembroke up by his foot, and stomped off to her room.

When she got to her room, the princess slammed
the door behind her and dropped Pembroke on
the floor.

Again Pembroke reminded Laura of the promise she
had made. Then, he jumped up onto the bed and
nestled himself into Laura's soft satin pillow.
The princess wasn't a bit happy.

The next morning Pembroke followed Laura everywhere she went.

Time passed, and Laura kept her promise to Pembroke. She played with him every day, let him eat from her plate, and let him sleep on her pillow at night–even though she didn't like the idea of sharing everything with a frog. Laura was so unhappy.

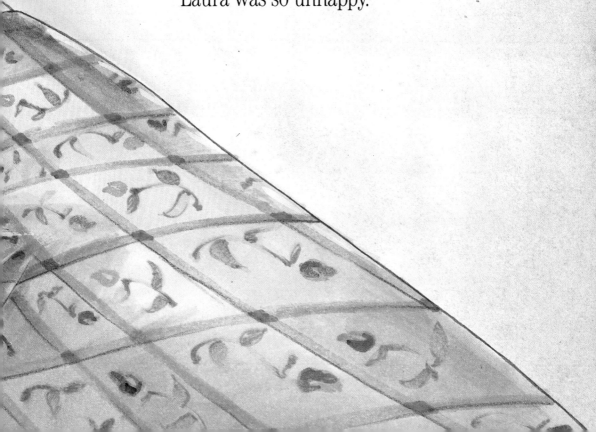

One night, the king and queen invited all of Laura's friends to dinner, hoping this would cheer her up.

As they entered the dining hall…there sat Pembroke at Laura's plate…with a napkin tied around his neck.

Laura's friends were quite surprised to see a frog sitting at the table. Laura tried to explain, but because they didn't understand at first, they teased Laura.

Laura's friends didn't mean to hurt her feelings, but their joking seemed cruel, and Laura was so upset.

She ran from the table to her room, Pembroke jumping along behind, trying to keep up with her.

When Laura reached her room, she turned around, grabbed Pembroke, and put him outside her bedroom window.

Pembroke looked in at Laura from outside the window, pressing his face against the glass. He called to her, but Laura was too angry to listen.

Just then, a large, hungry owl spied Pembroke on the window sill and swooped down. The owl thought Pembroke would make a delicious dinner.

Laura turned around and saw Pembroke just as the owl flew past him, almost touching the little frog with its claws. Pembroke fainted.

Laura ran to the window and brought Pembroke inside. He lay there in her hand, without moving.

Laura called to Pembroke, but he didn't answer.

And with that, Laura gave Pembroke a big kiss. Then slowly, he began to glow with a wonderful light. The light grew brighter and brighter, until suddenly, Pembroke turned from a little green frog…

…into a handsome prince!!

Pembroke explained that many years before a wicked witch had turned him into a frog. Only the kiss from a lovely princess could break the spell, and turn him back into a prince. Laura's kiss had done just that.

Pembroke and Laura remained the very best of friends. Then one day they made the greatest promise they could make to each other…when they married. He promised to love her, and she promised to love him, forever and ever. Which just goes to show you that first impressions can be very deceiving. Within every frog, there just might be a prince!

 *nd they all lived happily ever after.*